THIS LITTLE TIGER BOOK BELONGS TO:

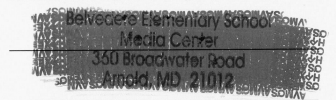

For Flora, Ron and Elaine
~J.S.

For Glen P.
~T.W.

This edition published 1997
First published in the United States 1996 by
Little Tiger Press,
12221 West Feerick Street, Wauwatosa, WI 53222
Originally published in Great Britain 1996 by
Magi Publications, London
Text © 1996 Julie Sykes
Illustrations © 1996 Tim Warnes
All rights reserved.
Library of Congress Cataloging-in-Publication Data.
Sykes, Julie.
I don't want to go to bed! / by Julie Sykes ; pictures by Tim Warnes.
p.   cm.
Summary : A little tiger that hates to go to bed scampers away
to visit some animal friends.
ISBN 1-888444-13-4 (pb)
[1. Bedtime–Fiction.   2. Tigers–Fiction.   3. Jungle animals–Fiction.]
I. Warnes, Tim. ill.   II. Title.
PZ7.S98325Iae 1996 [E]–dc20 96-14622 CIP AC
Printed and bound in Hong Kong
First U.S. paperback edition
1 3 5 7 9 10 8 6 4 2

I don't want to go to bed!

by Julie Sykes

Pictures by Tim Warnes

Little Tiger Press

Little Tiger did not like going to bed.
Every night when Mommy Tiger said,
"Bedtime!"
Little Tiger would say,
"But I don't *want* to go to bed!"

Little Tiger wouldn't let Mommy Tiger clean his face
and paws, and he wouldn't listen to his bedtime story.
One night Mommy Tiger lost her temper.
When Little Tiger said, "I don't want to go to bed!"
Mommy Tiger roared,
"ALL RIGHT THEN, YOU CAN STAY UP ALL NIGHT!"

Little Tiger couldn't believe his good luck.
He scampered off into the jungle before
Mommy Tiger could change her mind.

Little Tiger went to visit his
best friend, Little Lion.
When he arrived,
Little Lion was having
his ears washed.

"It's bedtime," growled Daddy Lion.
"Why are you still up?"
"I don't want to go to bed!" said Little Tiger,
and he skipped off into the jungle
before Daddy Lion could wash
his ears, too!

Little Tiger decided to visit his second
best friend, Little Hippo.
He found him splashing in the river,
having a bedtime bath.

"It's bedtime," bellowed Daddy Hippo.
"Why are you still up?"
"I don't want to go to bed!" said Little Tiger,
and he scurried off into the jungle before
Daddy Hippo could give him a bath, too!

Little Elephant was Little Tiger's third best friend.
He went to visit him next.
Little Elephant was not out playing.
He was in bed, listening to his bedtime story.

"It's bedtime," trumpeted Mommy Elephant.

"Why are you still up?"

"I don't want to go to bed!" said Little Tiger,
and he bounced off into the jungle before
Mommy Elephant could put him to bed, too!

Little Tiger thought he
would go and find
Little Monkey,
his fourth best friend.
But he found Mommy
Monkey first. She put a finger
to her lips and whispered,
"Little Monkey is fast asleep.
Why are you still up?"

"I don't want to go to bed!"
Little Tiger whispered back.
Quickly he tiptoed into the
jungle before Mommy Monkey
made him fall asleep, too!

Little Tiger didn't know where to go next. It was the
first time he had been in the jungle so late by himself.
Even the sun had gone to bed!
Suddenly it seemed very dark.
What was that?

Little Tiger looked up
and saw . . .

. . . two very large yellow eyes
staring back at him!

The eyes belonged to a bush baby.
"Shouldn't you be in bed?" she asked.
"I don't want to go to bed,"
said Little Tiger
bravely. "*You* haven't!"
"That's because I go to
bed when the sun rises,"
said Bush Baby.

Little Tiger couldn't imagine going to bed in the sunshine! He shivered and thought how cold and dark it was in the jungle at night.

"I'm going to take you home," said Bush Baby.
"Your mommy will be worried about you."
"I don't want to go home! I don't want to go to bed!"
said Little Tiger. But he didn't want to be left alone
in the dark either.

So Little Tiger followed Bush Baby through the jungle.
He was glad of her big bright eyes, showing him the
way back home.
"We're almost there," said Bush Baby, as Little Tiger's
steps became slower and slower.

"I don't want to go to . . ." said Little Tiger sleepily,
dragging his paws.
"Oh, there you are," said Mommy Tiger,
"just in time for bed!"

"I don't want to . . ." yawned Little Tiger,
and he fell fast asleep!
Mommy Tiger tucked him in
and turned to Bush Baby . . .

. . . but the den was empty.
Bush Baby had disappeared into
the jungle before Mommy Tiger
could tuck *her* in, too!

Some more books from
LITTLE TIGER PRESS
for you to enjoy

ROBBIE RABBIT AND THE LITTLE ONES

by Julie Sykes and pictures by Catherine Walters
ISBN 1-888444-11-8 $4.95
When Robbie Rabbit plays hide-and-seek with his little brothers and sisters
he can't find them anywhere—but he does find something far more scary!
"An endearing story which children will love to hear and later read"
—*Children's Book Review Service*

WHAT IF?

by A. H. Benjamin and pictures by Jane Chapman
ISBN 1-888444-14-2 $5.95
When a kangaroo arrives at Buttercup Farm all the other animals are very
worried. What does a kangaroo do? What if she takes over their jobs?
Sunny artwork highlights this memorable tale.

LAZY OZZIE

by Michael Coleman and pictures by Gwyneth Williamson
ISBN 1-888444-12-6 $4.95
Ozzie is too lazy to learn how to fly, and he thinks up a clever plan to make
his mother believe that he can—but is she really fooled?
"Skillful watercolor and ink illustrations add bounce, but never get in the way
of the story."—*Kirkus Reviews*

LITTLE TIGER PRESS
12221 West Feerick Street, Wauwatosa, WI 53222